MY FAVORITE PRESIDENT

AND OTHER STORIES

STARSCAPE BOOKS BY DAVID LUBAR

Novels

Flip
Hidden Talents
True Talents

Monsterrific Tales

Hyde and Shriek
The Vanishing Vampire
The Unwilling Witch
The Wavering Werewolf
The Gloomy Ghost
The Bully Bug

Nathan Abercrombie, Accidental Zombie series

My Rotten Life
Dead Guy Spy
Goop Soup
The Big Stink
Enter the Zombie

Story Collections

Attack of the Vampire Weenies and Other Warped and Creepy Tales

The Battle of the Red Hot Pepper Weenies and Other Warped and Creepy Tales

Beware the Ninja Weenies and Other Warped and Creepy Tales

Check Out the Library Weenies and Other Warped and Creepy Tales

The Curse of the Campfire Weenies and Other Warped and Creepy Tales

In the Land of the Lawn Weenies and Other Warped and Creepy Tales

Invasion of the Road Weenies and Other Warped and Creepy Tales

Strikeout of the Bleacher Weenies and Other Warped and Creepy Tales

Wipeout of the Wireless Weenies and Other Warped and Creepy Tales

Teeny Weenies: The Boy Who Cried Wool and Other Stories

Teeny Weenies: Freestyle Frenzy and Other Stories

Teeny Weenies: The Intergalactic Petting Zoo and Other Stories

MY FAVORITE
PRESIDENT
AND OTHER STORIES

DAVID LUBAR

ILLUSTRATED BY BILL MAYER

STARSCAPE

A TOM DOHERTY ASSOCIATES BOOK
NEW YORK

MY FAVORITE PRESIDENT AND OTHER STORIES

Copyright © 2019 by David Lubar

Illustrations copyright © 2019 by Bill Mayer

A Starscape Book
Published by Tom Doherty Associates
120 Broadway
New York, NY 10271

www.tor-forge.com

The Library of Congress Cataloging-in-Publication Data is available upon request.

ISBN 978-1-250-17358-4 (hardcover)
ISBN 978-1-250-18782-6 (ebook)

Our books may be purchased in bulk for promotional, educational, or business use. Please contact your local bookseller or the Macmillan Corporate and Premium Sales Department at 1-800-221-7945, extension 5442, or by email at MacmillanSpecialMarkets@macmillan.com.

First Edition: September 2019

Printed in the United States of America

0 9 8 7 6 5 4 3 2 1

*For my good friends Danny and Kim Adlerman,
whose kindness, generosity, and good spirits
make the world a better place.*

CONTENTS

MY FAVORITE PRESIDENT

had to write a report on the greatest American president. We'd gotten the assignment on Monday. It was due on Friday. Right now, it's Thursday, an hour before bedtime. And, yeah, I'm just about to start my report. I kept putting it off. And my parents, who normally ask me about homework, had been real busy. Mom was starting a new job. Dad was traveling.

Did I mention it had to be three pages long? Right now, I didn't even have three words. Okay. I couldn't put it off any longer. I had to get started. I figured it would be easy to do George Washington. I mean, he helped America get independence. He was the father of our country.

I sat at my desk and started typing.

George Washington was the greatest American president . . .

I paused to decide what to say next.

"Bad choice."

The words startled me enough that I let out a shout.

"Whoa!"

I looked up at the guy standing next to me. Then I looked farther up, because he was *really* tall. And he was wearing a hat that made him look even taller.

"Lincoln?" I asked.

He smiled and nodded.

I managed to ask the obvious question. "What are you doing here?"

"Trying to keep you from making a mistake," Lincoln said. "Don't pick George. He wasn't all that great."

"Are you kidding?" I felt I had to defend my choice. "He was the father of our country."

"He had wooden teeth," Lincoln said.

"That's a myth," I said. We'd learned about that in school.

Lincoln shook his head. "It's not a myth. You should have heard him try to talk. I had a really hard time understanding him."

"You didn't talk with him," I said. "He died before you were born."

"Are you sure about that, Blake?" he asked.

"Yeah. I'm positive!" I blurted out. But then I paused. I wasn't totally sure at all. But it sounded right. I ran some historical dates through my mind. The revolution was in 1776. I had no idea how old Washington was at the time or how long he lived. The Civil War was somewhere in the middle of the 1800s. I could never remember exactly when. And I had no idea how old Lincoln was at that time.

I realized none of that mattered. "Who cares about his teeth? That's not important. And it doesn't take away anything from him being great. Really, who was greater?"

Lincoln pointed at himself. Then he listed a string of his accomplishments. Somewhere along the way—it was a long list—my mind wandered and stumbled right into one thought that would totally end this conversation.

"Mr. Lincoln," I said, holding up my hand to stop him from talking.

"Yes?"

"You say you're the greatest president?" I asked.

"Absolutely," he said.

"But I think that rules you out. Anyone who is so full of himself that he thinks he's great probably isn't as great as he thinks he is, especially if he thinks he's the greatest of all." As the words spilled out, I realized that was a pretty deep thought. And a true one. I waited to see whether Lincoln would try to argue with me. I knew he was a great debater. But I felt my argument was solid.

Lincoln laughed. "Nicely stated, Blake. And you're right. If I really believed that I was the greatest, I wouldn't be great at all."

Now, I was confused. "Wait. So you don't believe you're the greatest president?"

"No. Not at all." His smiled faded. "I was just a man trying to do his best at a very difficult time in our history."

"So why did you say all that stuff?" I asked.

"I was just messing with you. George wanted to thank you himself for picking him. But he's pretty busy right now. There are a ton of kids writing about him this evening. So he asked me to help him out."

"Oh . . ."

"And I am a bit of a joker, which you would know if you'd studied me at all," he said.

"Maybe next year," I said.

"Maybe?" he asked.

"Either you or Herbert Hoover," I said, picking a random president I knew absolutely nothing about.

Lincoln stared at me and frowned. "Hoover? Are you kidding me?"

"Yup." I let out a laugh. "You aren't the only joker in the room." And then I got back to work, because I wanted to get good grades so maybe I could grow up to be president, too.

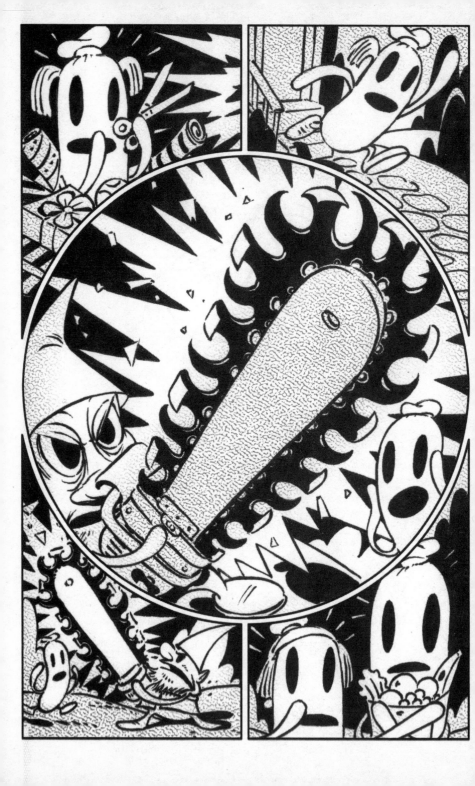

HOME WRECKERS

Imagine a thousand pencil sharpeners grinding the tips of a thousand pencils. Now, imagine that all the pencils are made of steel. Then totally forget what that would sound like, because what I heard was a whole lot worse.

I was up in my room, sitting on the floor, wrapping the Christmas presents I'd bought for my parents. That's when the screech shot through my closed window. The floor shook beneath me. I stood up, trying to figure out what was going on. The noise was somewhere outside. I was alone in the house. My parents had just headed out for the super-market.

I ran out the front door. The sound got louder when I reached the porch. I stopped and listened. It seemed to be coming from the back. I went through the gate in the fence and headed for the backyard.

There was someone—no, some*thing*—sawing away at the foundation of the house, right at the corner. The thing was about two feet tall. He was shaped like a person, as far as having arms, legs, and a head, but his skin reminded me of that white bark that peels off birch trees, and his limbs were as thin as sticks.

Despite that, he must have been incredibly strong, because the saw was almost as long as he was tall. And it was a serious saw. Not one of those little plug-in ones my dad has in the garage. This was the kind of gasoline-powered beast that can cut through steel and concrete. I saw proof of this in the slash he'd already made through the cinder blocks that supported the house. Cement dust coated the ground at his feet.

The feet, by the way, were bare. Above them, he wore knee-length brown pants and a brown vest.

"Hey! Stop!" My shout was no match for the roar of the saw's engine or the screech of its blade, and I'm the loudest girl in my class. At least, that's what my teacher claims.

The thing kept cutting. He had sawed into the corner of the foundation and started to move along the back of the house. He obviously hadn't heard me. I didn't want to get close enough to tap him on the shoulder. If I startled him and he turned, that saw would swing in my direction.

I looked for something to throw to get his attention. Just then, he glanced over his shoulder.

I shouted again. I was still drowned out, but I figured he would at least see my mouth move. I waved my hands for added effect.

That worked.

The thing pulled the saw from the cut. The awful screech dropped to the tiger-purr rumble of an idling engine. "What do you want?" he asked. He had a pretty deep voice for something so small.

"Are you kidding? You're cutting up my house!"

The thing shrugged. "Seems fair. You cut down my house yesterday."

That was crazy. "No, I didn't."

He glared at me. "Yes, you did. You cut it down, dragged it away from where it belonged, tied it on top of a car, and drove off, singing cheerful songs like you didn't have a care in the world or a stump where your home used to be. It's a good thing I was out at the time."

"You're definitely out of your mind," I said. "All I did yesterday was go get a tree."

"All you did?" The thing stared at me and spread out his hands, one of which still clutched the saw, as if to say, "*Now do you get it?*"

"Wait . . ." I thought back. "The tree?" We'd gone to one of those places where you cut down your own Christmas tree. I'd thought it was a lot of extra work, when there were dozens of places where you could buy a tree that was already cut, and lots of stores where you could buy a fake one that would last forever, but Dad seemed to think the experience of hiking through muddy fields and selecting the perfect spruce would make a great childhood memory for me.

"That tree was my home," the creature said.

"Your home?" I tried to imagine living in a tree. That was fine for birds and squirrels. But not for anything with two arms and two legs. "What *are* you?"

"A tree gnome," he said.

"I've never heard of that," I said.

"What's your name?" he asked.

"Becky Dryson."

"Never heard of you. And yet, you exist." He revved up the saw. "If you'll excuse me, I have a lot of work to do. I'll say this for you people—you build sturdy homes."

"But you can't do that. That's my house. I live there."

"You cut mine down and dragged it off," he said. "I'm just returning the favor."

"So take yours back," I said.

"I can't. You killed it."

He went back to sawing. I went back to shouting. Only one of us made any progress.

I gave up shouting and followed him as he made his way around the house. At several points, sparks flew as he cut through power lines. At one point, water gushed. I guess it was a good thing we didn't have natural gas.

He finished his cut back at the corner where he'd started. The house gave a small shudder when he pulled the saw free, as if it were just now realizing that things had changed in a big way.

He killed the engine. The sudden silence added to the strangeness of the scene. He put his arm through a strap and slung the saw over his shoulder. I followed him again as he walked to the front of the house.

"Please don't . . . ," I said.

He ignored me, spat on his palms, grabbed two of the porch rails, and tugged. The house slid off the foundation. He dragged it down the front lawn, pretty much stripping the grass, then headed up the street in the direction of the Christmas tree farm. While nowhere near as terrible as the screech of the saw, the scrape of the concrete against the road was pretty awful.

I looked down at our basement, which was all that was left of our house. It was beyond weird seeing the clutter of boxes and old furniture from above. I didn't move. I guess I was in shock.

My parents were beyond shocked when

they got home. They stood there by the car, holding bags of groceries, staring at the empty space where the house had been.

After a long silence, Dad gave the bag in his hands a sad look and said, "The ice cream is going to melt."

"I was going to mop the kitchen floor," Mom said.

It took a while before they noticed me. Once they seemed able to listen, I told them what had happened. They didn't believe me. They decided that whatever had really happened was so terrible that I had created a fantasy to explain things to myself.

For a month or two, they seemed to expect me to suddenly remember the truth and give them a satisfactory explanation. After a while, they accepted that the disappearance of our house would remain a mystery to them.

All of this happened nearly ten months ago. We live in an apartment now. Everything was fine until this morning, when Dad sprang his big surprise.

"I have great plans for Halloween," he said. "We're going to go to the pumpkin patch and pick our own pumpkin. The biggest one we can find. We'll cut it right off the vine."

I shuddered at the word *cut,* pictured Dad slicing his way through a thick, woody pumpkin stem with a handsaw, and wondered what sort of creature might make his home in a pumpkin. I really didn't want to find out. But I had a feeling I would. And I was pretty sure I wouldn't like it.

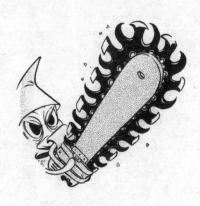

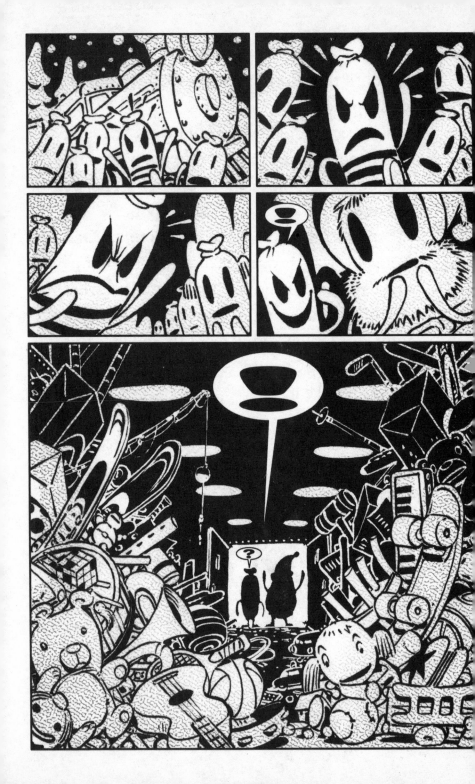

POLAR
OPPOSITES

Peter had always thought it was just a story. His mom had read the picture book to him often enough. But there it was, big as a dream and dark as a nightmare. The train. The one and only. Loaded to bursting with nice kids who minded their manners and always remembered to say *please* and *thank you*. Filled with kids from engine to caboose and on its way to the top of the world.

"They don't stand a chance against me," Peter muttered as he sneaked into a car near the back of the train. "Hey," he shouted at the smallest kid he could find, "that's my seat! Get out of it!"

The kid scurried away, whimpering.

Peter sat and enjoyed the ride.

When the train arrived at the North Pole, Peter pushed his way to the head of the line. The Man himself was there, passing out candy canes. Santa winked at Peter, put his arm around him, and said, "I've been looking for someone like you. Got anything important going on at home?"

"Nope," Peter said. "Nothing at all."

"Good. Follow me."

Santa led Peter through the workshop. "Here you go," Santa said, herding Peter into a room so vast that the far wall seemed no larger than a postage stamp. The whole room was lined with empty shelves, but that's not what caught Peter's attention. It was the amazing stack of treasures on the floor that made him gasp.

"Wow," Peter said, his eyes sweeping across

the floor. "It looks like every toy in the world is here."

"Yup," Santa said. "That's 10,837,459 toys. One each of every toy ever made. And it's all yours."

"Holy cow!" Peter said.

"There's just one small rule," Santa told him.

"What's that?" Peter asked.

Santa looked embarrassed. "It's not really my idea. But Mrs. Claus insists on it."

"So what's the rule?" Peter asked again.

Santa pointed to the empty shelves that lined the enormous room. And then, he pointed to the 10,837,459 toys scattered across the floor. "No dinner until you pick up your room. See you later, pal," he said as he stepped outside and bolted the door.

As far as anyone knows, Peter is still at it.

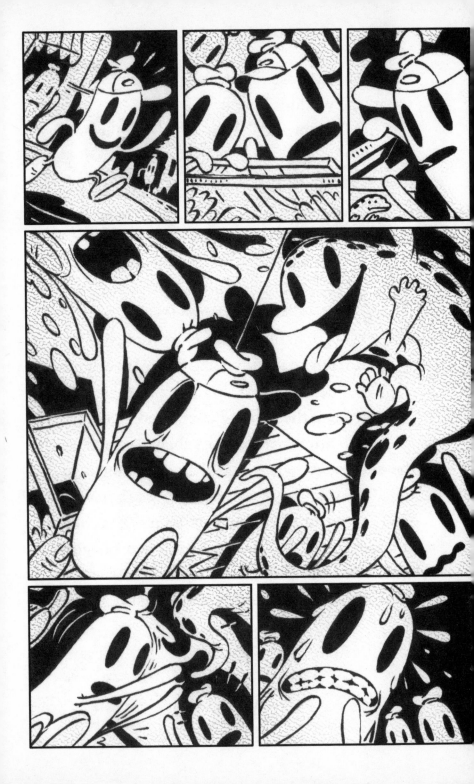

WE'RE OFF TO
SEE THE LIZARD

The doorbell rang again. Kelly knew what was coming next. "Could you get that, Kelly?" her older brother, Jeff, asked.

"Sure, but this is the last time." She was growing tired of answering the bell. She was growing especially tired of all of Jeff's friends coming over. She went down the hall and opened the door, then shivered as a blast of winter air ran across her face and arms.

"Hi," Rickie Walton said. "I heard Jeff got a real cool lizard. Can I see it?"

Kelly nodded, then pointed over her shoulder with her thumb. She was also tired of talking to all of Jeff's friends.

"Thanks," Rickie said, rushing down the hall.

"Sure," Kelly muttered. She wandered back toward the family room. It was getting so crowded, she didn't even see any place where she could sit. There were kids on the couch and on both chairs. Everyone was coming to see the stupid lizard. Six kids had come over so far, and Kelly was sure that more were on their way. She wouldn't have minded so much, but Jeff hadn't even given her a chance to look at the lizard. He was far too busy showing it to all his friends. Not that she was interested in the silly thing, but it would have been nice of him to ask.

"That's cool!" one kid was saying.

"Real awesome. Take it out," another said.

Jeff shook his head. "I'm not supposed to."

Cries of "Oh, come on" and "Just for a little bit" burst from the crowd.

Jeff shrugged and opened the top of the

cage. He reached down and grabbed the lizard.

He shouldn't do that, Kelly thought. She knew Jeff was only supposed to let the lizard out in his room. Kelly remembered how their mom had made Jeff promise he would take good care of his new pet.

"Get it!"

The shout shook the thoughts right out of her mind. Kelly looked across the room just in time to see Jeff diving toward the couch. Kids were jumping all over. One kid was trying to crawl under the couch after the lizard. Another was climbing on top of the couch to get away from it.

Kelly didn't panic. She walked across the room and closed the door so the lizard couldn't get out.

"Oh, this is bad," Jeff said. "I'd better get it back or I'm in trouble." He wiped his forehead with the back of his hand. He was starting to sweat.

"I can help," Kelly said, feeling sorry for him.

"No, thanks," Jeff said. "I can do it myself." He reached beneath the couch. The lizard ran out from under there and dashed up the wall. Jeff raced after it. He reached toward the wall, but the lizard scooted out of his grasp again.

Kelly just watched. She had no plans to help after Jeff had turned down her offer. The lizard ran across the wall to the corner of the room. It was lower now.

"Try sneaking up on it," someone suggested.

Jeff moved like a cat stalking a chipmunk. He got really close to the lizard. He reached out.

Zip! The lizard skittered from his clutches.

Kelly fanned herself. It was really getting warm with the door closed and all the people in the room.

"Help me," Jeff said to Rickie. "You go

from that side and I'll go from this side."

"Okay," Rickie said.

Kelly watched. She doubted they would have any luck capturing the slithery critter. It had speed, reflexes, and instinct on its side.

The lizard sat motionless on the wall between the boys. Jeff and Rickie inched toward it. They both reached out at once. The lizard shot up the wall, and Jeff and Rickie ran into each other.

Kelly shook her head. They'd never catch it. But she wasn't going to offer any more help. A drop of sweat rolled down her nose. She flicked it off. *It would be nice to open a window and get a blast of winter air,* she thought. It was so hot.

Winter air . . . The thought and feel of it tickled Kelly's mind.

"That's it!" she shouted.

Everyone in the room turned and stared at her. Even the lizard seemed to look her way.

"What?" Jeff asked.

"The heat. That's the problem," Kelly said.

Jeff seemed puzzled. Kelly saw that she would have to explain. "Lizards are cold-blooded. The hotter it is, the more active they get. And the colder it is—"

"The less active," Jeff said, finishing the thought for her.

Kelly nodded. "Exactly. All we have to do is cool the room. Let's turn off the heat." She went over to the thermostat and adjusted the controls while Jeff opened the window. Cold air swept into the room, pushing the curtains aside as it blew through the screen.

They watched the lizard. Its tail was twitching. Bit by bit, as the room grew colder, the tail slowed.

"Now?" Jeff asked when the lizard stopped moving altogether.

"Try it," Kelly said.

Jeff started to reach for the lizard, then pulled his hand back. He smiled. "You do it. You haven't had a real chance to see it yet."

"Thanks." Kelly reached toward the lizard. It didn't move. Gently, she took it from the wall and cradled its dry body in her hands. After a moment, she returned it to its cage. As she closed the lid, Jeff's friends started clapping and cheering.

"Good thinking," one of them said.

"Smart going," another told her.

Kelly smiled, then said, "I have to admit it was a cool idea." She went to close the window. It was pretty cold in the room—cold enough to see her breath. But the funny thing was, she didn't feel cold at all. At the moment, she felt happy and warm.

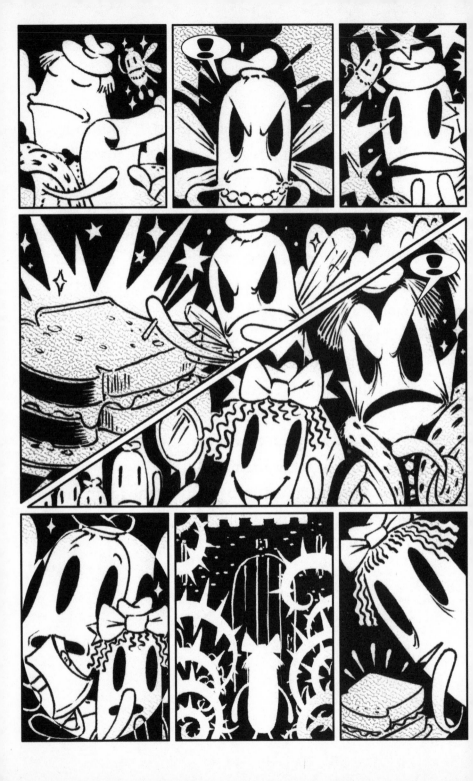

BEAUTY AND
THE BEEF

There once was a prince who was terribly handsome. He was also terribly proud. And not terribly bright. So when he was invited to the fairy ball, he made the mistake of saying, "No, thank you. Fairies are silly little creatures who chatter away all day about silly little things, and fairy balls are unbearably boring. The food is terrible, too."

He might not have had a problem if he'd said that to his squire, or to his horse (who was actually quite bright), but he said this in front of the Fairy Queen, who placed a curse on him. She could have turned him into a frog, or a mule, or removed his ability to talk, but she was already having a bad day and wanted to give him an especially terrible punishment. So she turned him into a roast beef sandwich. And not a lovely and desirable sandwich with beautifully crusty bread, thick pieces of freshly carved rare beef, a fresh leaf of frilly green lettuce, and a slice or two from a red, ripe garden tomato. No, he was pretty much a dried-up, unappealing slab of gristly meat on two stale pieces of crumbly bread. No mayo. No mustard.

"You will remain that way until someone truly loves you," the Fairy Queen said, placing the prince on the banquet table in his castle.

"Help," the prince said.

Nobody heard him. He had a very quiet voice, made even quieter by his current lack of vocal cords, lungs, or a tongue. Nobody paid any attention to him or knew what he had become, since sandwiches had not yet been invented by people, though fairies had been making them for centuries.

There once was also a fair maiden named Merrigayle, who was the most beautiful young lass in the land. An evil queen heard rumors about her. The queen felt she herself was the most beautiful person in the land. So she summoned her huntsman and said, "Find that fair maiden and kill her."

"Yes, ma'am," the huntsman said. Like most huntsmen, he was not an evil person. So when he found the fair maiden, he took her into the woods but didn't kill her.

(There was another beautiful young lass who ate a poisoned apple and fell into a deep sleep. But she slept through the whole story and will not be mentioned again. Let's get back to our current lass.)

Merrigayle wandered through the

woods until she reached an old castle over-grown with weeds and thorns. She found her way inside, hoping to get some food.

There was something odd sitting on the banquet table. It seemed to be a stack of bread and meat. Merrigayle stared at it. "What are you?" she asked.

"A prince," the sandwich said.

Merrigayle, who had not expected an answer, stepped back and gasped. "You can talk!"

"Of course I can," the sandwich said. "I've been talking all my life."

"But what are you?" Merrigayle asked.

"A prince," the prince said, once again.

"I've never seen a prince like you before," Merrigayle said.

"I believe I've been cursed," he said.

Merrigayle reached out and poked the top of the sandwich with one finger. "Who cursed you?" she asked.

"The Fairy Queen," he said. "She turned me into this thing. And now I have to wait until someone comes along who truly loves me."

"There's not much here to love," Merrigayle said.

The sandwich, somehow, sighed. "I know. It's a pretty powerful curse. Perhaps you could take a small nibble out of me. I could be so tasty you'd fall in love."

"Ew . . . ," Merrigayle said, studying the sandwich. That didn't appeal to her.

"Please," the prince said. "It might be my only hope. I haven't had many visitors. Actually, I haven't had a single one before you." He made a peculiar sound.

Merrigayle realized he was sobbing. "Stop. You'll get soggy. And then you will definitely be unlovable."

The prince sniffed and snuffled but managed to stop sobbing.

"I don't see any part of you that looks tasty at all," Merrigayle said.

"I suppose not," the prince said.

But Merrigayle, who really did have a pure heart and a weakness for people in need, picked up the sandwich and took the tiniest possible nibble.

The sandwich tasted amazing.

Had the prince bothered to learn something about fairies instead of mocking them, he might have found that fairies are incapable of making a bad sandwich. In fact, all their food is unbelievably delicious.

He would also have discovered this if he'd been open-minded enough to go to the ball.

Unfortunately, he knew none of this.

More unfortunately, Merrigayle was just learning it.

The sandwich was truly amazing.

It was actually irresistible.

And soon enough, it was nothing but a tasty memory.

"Sorry," Merrigayle whispered when she

realized there was nothing left of the prince for her to love.

No longer hungry, Merrigayle left the castle.

Unlike the prince, she lived happily ever after.

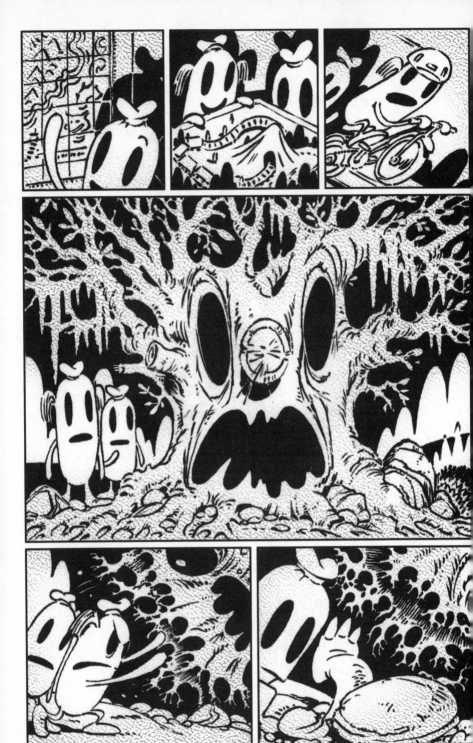

I'VE GOT MY EYE ON YOU

ere, there be dragons.

That's what it says on the map my brother, Dylan, has on the wall over his bed. It's an old-fashioned map from way back when they didn't know much about the earth. They thought there were dragons in the ocean. I wish that were true. It would be cool to see a dragon. From a distance, of course.

Dylan likes ancient history. I like old stuff, too, but not anywhere near that old. I like trains from the 1800s and 1900s. I have a cool setup in the basement. My main layout is HO scale, which is one eighty-seventh real size, but I have stuff at every scale from tiny to pretty large.

Anyhow, the reason I mentioned dragons is that we ran into a different monster, and not one I wanted to meet.

We'd been riding our bikes on the trail through Bryer Woods when Dylan skidded off the path and wiped out.

"You okay?" I asked when I pulled up next to him.

He looked down like he was checking his body for broken pieces, then said, "Yeah. I'm fine. But I think this tree has had it."

He tapped the old, dead tree that had stopped his slide. It creaked a lot and tilted a bit. It looked like it was just about ready to fall over.

"Might as well help it out," I said. So we gave the tree a shove. Hey, that's what guys do. We break things.

The tree fell hard and slid down the hillside into a gully. It took a couple of boulders with it.

"Cool," I said, staring down the hill at the mini landslide we'd created.

"What's that?" Dylan asked.

Something slithered out from the hole where the biggest boulder had been.

"Snake?" I guessed.

"Snakes don't have fingers," Dylan said. "That's an arm."

"Arms don't come that big," I said. Even from a distance, I could tell that whatever we were looking at was part of something huge.

It turned out it was an arm. We discovered that when the rest of it burst out onto the hillside.

It was a giant. I saw the other arm break through. And then the head came out, facing away from us.

"It's huge!" Dylan said. It was all the way

out of the hole now. It looked like it was at least seven or eight feet tall and really broad.

"Enormous." I glanced over my shoulder at my bike. "We should get out of here," I said.

"I want to see what it looks like close up," Dylan said.

I took a step away from him. "I don't think that's a good idea."

Dylan obviously thought otherwise. "Hey! Big guy! Over here!" Dylan jumped up and down and waved his arms.

The giant turned around and stared back at us with one enormous eye in the center of its head.

"Cyclops!" I said.

"Cool," Dylan said. "I read about them in *The Odyssey*. I never thought they were real."

"Not cool," I said as the cyclops let out a roar of rage and charged toward us. "Run!"

I dashed for my bike, but I waited long enough to make sure Dylan got back on his. We raced down the path. The cyclops chased after us, knocking over any trees that got in its way. It was fast, but we managed to keep ahead.

Dylan pedaled up beside me when we reached the road. "What are we going to do?" he asked.

"Stay ahead of it," I said.

"Forever?" he asked.

That was a good question. "We can go home and lock ourselves inside. Then we can call for help," I suggested.

A rock went flying past my head. I guess the cyclops had thrown it.

"I don't think our front door will do much good," I said.

"Wait! I have an idea," Dylan said. "But I need to get home ahead of you. Can you slow down a bit?"

I checked over my shoulder. "Are you kidding?"

"No. I'm serious. I just need to get there a minute or two ahead of you," he said.

"Why?" I asked.

"There's no time to explain," he said. "Just trust me. Okay?"

"Okay," I said. "Go for it." If you can't trust your brother, who can you trust?

It wasn't easy, but I slowed down until I felt the cyclops was getting too close. Then I increased my speed just enough so he wouldn't get any closer. Dylan pulled ahead. I hoped he knew what he was doing. I couldn't even guess what he had in mind. But if it didn't work, we'd be in big trouble.

I was getting tired. And I was slowing down. I knew I couldn't stay ahead of the cyclops for much longer. Even so, I took the long way home, going all the way around the neighborhood to give Dylan more time.

Finally, with the cyclops getting so close I could almost feel his breath on my neck, I turned onto our street. Dylan was in the driveway, standing behind several rows of stuff that looked familiar. As I got closer, I saw what they were and screamed, "Hey! What are you doing with my trains?"

Dylan ignored me. He raised his arms and growled like an angry bear. He was clutching my favorite caboose. I was close enough now to see that he'd lined up a bunch of trains, with the largest-scale ones in front and the smaller ones in back. It looked a little bit like they were spread out over a large area.

Dylan roared again. I couldn't believe he thought he could scare the cyclops this way.

I heard a cry of fright from behind me. The cyclops had stopped chasing me. He was staring at Dylan now like my brother was some sort of monster.

Dylan stomped his foot and let out the loudest roar yet. He waved the caboose in his hand and then crushed it.

"Hey!" I shouted.

The cyclops turned and ran away, heading back toward the woods.

I staggered off my bike and walked over to Dylan.

"How . . . ?"

I was too puzzled and out of breath to talk, but I guess he knew what I was asking.

"I made myself into a giant," Dylan said. He held his hand right in front of my face and then slowly pulled it away. "You need two eyes to see depth," he said as his hand grew smaller.

"So he thought you were a giant," I said. "Because everything got smaller and smaller in front of you."

"That's how it looks," he said.

"That was brilliant," I said.

"I know."

"But you didn't have to ruin my caboose," I said.

Dylan flashed me a guilty grin. "Probably not. Want to go back to the Bryer Woods?"

I shook my head. "Definitely not."

And we didn't.

DROP THE BALL

For the first eight years of her life, Bonnie's New Year's Eve experience went like this. Her parents tucked her in at her normal bedtime, whispered, "Happy New Year, young lady," to her, and went off to enjoy a party in the living room with a group of their friends.

The same thing happened for the first seven years of Lisa's life. She was Bonnie's younger sister.

But the year when Bonnie turned nine, she decided that she wasn't going to be left out any longer.

"We're going to the party," she told Lisa the morning of New Year's Eve.

"Why?" Lisa asked.

"I heard they watch this giant glittery ball drop while everyone counts down, and then they all cheer," Bonnie said. "I'm tired of missing out on everything."

"It sounds kind of boring," Lisa said.

"It sounds amazing," Bonnie said. "I'm going to sneak down right before midnight and watch. You should come, too."

"Sure," Lisa said. "Why not? If it's amazing, I won't miss out. And if it isn't amazing, I can kid you about it. Either way, I win."

Bonnie hadn't thought about it that way. But she was sure it would be amazing. That night, she let her parents tuck her in and whisper what they always whispered. And she closed her eyes. As soon as she heard them leave her room, she opened her eyes and double-checked that she'd set the alarm on her phone for 11:55. It turned out that wasn't necessary. She was so excited, she didn't fall asleep. All night, she listened to the sounds from below. People were talking and laughing and even singing. As midnight approached, things got quieter.

The alarm startled her—not because she was asleep but because she'd forgotten all about setting it. She turned it off, woke Lisa, then crept down the stairs to the living room.

Her parents and their friends were all there. And they were all fast asleep. On the couches and in the chairs, they were sprawled out. Some were snoring. Some were tossing and turning a bit. But nobody was watching the countdown on the TV. Bonnie stared from face to face in disbelief. She helped herself to a potato chip from the bowl on the table. She watched the TV. At midnight, the ball dropped.

"That's it?" Lisa asked.

"I guess so," Bonnie said. "It looks like you were right."

"Yeah," she said. "I guess I was. I wish I'd been wrong. It would have been nice to see something exciting."

"But look on the bright side," Bonnie said. "It's a new year. A brand-new year. I'm going to make the most of it."

"Me, too," Lisa said. "Is there anything special you want to do this year?"

"Sure," Bonnie said. "Lots of things. But I also know one thing I don't want to do with this year."

"What's that?" Lisa asked.

Bonnie pointed to the sleeping adults. "When the time comes, I don't want to sit around and fall asleep waiting to watch it end."

UNDER THE RAINBOW

A rainbow!" Tad screamed, flinging his arm out to point at the sky. He and his twin brother, Rufus, had been sitting on rocks by a river. They'd just escaped from the third day of a boring family reunion that had brought them and their parents all the way from Madison, New Jersey, to the Greek island of Naxos.

"Big whoop," Rufus muttered. "We see them all the time."

"But they're always far away," Tad said. "Look at this one. It's close! Real close."

"So?" Rufus asked.

"So we can find the pot of gold." Tad pointed toward the spot where the rainbow disappeared behind the woods. "If you go to the end of the rainbow, that's where leprechauns hide their pot of gold. Everybody knows that. And today is St. Patrick's Day, so there absolutely have to be leprechauns all over the place."

"Maybe in Ireland," Rufus said. "But we're in Greece."

"It doesn't matter. Not today." Tad yanked at his brother's shoulder. "Come on. I'll need your help carrying the pot."

"How big do you think it is?" Rufus asked.

"I don't know. But it doesn't matter. It will be gold! Any gold is more gold than we have. We can buy everything we've ever wanted. And even everything we've never wanted." He started to drag his brother toward the end of the rainbow.

"Quit tugging. I'm coming." Rufus rose to his feet, sighed, and trotted off after Tad.

They went over the river (by way of a bridge) and through the woods (by way of a path), skipped past their grandmother's house, and kept angling toward where the rainbow seemed to touch ground on the far side of a hill past gently rolling fields of farmland.

By now, Rufus, who didn't much enjoy exercise, was huffing and puffing. And Tad, who didn't much enjoy anything other than dreams of wealth, was panting like a dog in the desert.

"Almost there . . . ," Tad gasped.

They pushed onward. As they reached the foot of the hill, Rufus let out a scream. It was his turn to fling out his arm and point.

Tad, who had no breath left, let out a smaller scream that sounded more like a cough. But his eyes grew wide as he stared at the statue that stood on the slope just above them. It was a life-size sculpture of a man who himself, based on the way his face was scrunched up, was letting out a horrifying scream. The man pointed with one hand at whatever had terrified him. Both boys looked where the finger was aimed but saw nothing frightening.

That didn't calm Rufus down at all. "Let's get out of here," he said.

"Nonsense," Tad said after he'd managed to catch his breath. "That's just put here to scare people off from getting the gold. Which proves there has to be gold there."

"You think?" Rufus asked.

"I'm sure of it," Tad said. "Leprechauns are tricky. Look, there's another scary one." He pointed to a second statue. This time, it was of a screaming woman, holding her hands out as if she were trying to stop a charging bull.

"That's awful," Rufus said.

"But it shows we're on the right track," Tad said. "The leprechauns wouldn't try to scare us off if there were nothing to protect."

When they reached the top of the hill, Tad gasped again. But this time, it wasn't from fear. It was from wonder.

"It's huge . . . ," he said.

"Enormous . . . ," Rufus said.

It was both those things and more. About fifty yards past the foot of the hill, beyond a dozen more statues, at the far end of the rainbow, sat a gigantic pot, taller than the twins and filled to overflowing with shiny gold coins.

"We're going to have to make a lot of trips," Tad said. "But it will be worth it. We'll be able to buy anything we want."

"Maybe we should buy a wagon first," Rufus said.

"Good idea," Tad said. He raced down the hill, drawn by the treasure that lay ahead. As he got closer, he saw a small man dressed in a green vest, green shirt, and green pants, sitting on a rock, facing the gold. Green hair jutted down from the back of his green cap.

"That's the leprechaun," Tad said.

"I know," Rufus said, catching up with his brother. "Think he'll try to stop us?"

"I don't think he can," Tad said. "If you find the gold, you get to keep it. That's the rule."

"You're right," the leprechaun said without turning to face the twins.

"You won't stop us?" Tad asked.

"I wouldn't dream of it," the leprechaun said.

"Hey, you don't sound Irish," Rufus said.

"That's because I'm a mixie," the leprechaun said.

"Pixie?" Tad asked.

"No, no, no. Not one of them," the leprechaun said, keeping his back toward them. "Mixie. I'm only leprechaun on my father's side. I'm Greek on my mother's side, descended from Gaia. I'm a beautiful mythical mix. Get it? Mixie."

Had the twins paid a bit more attention in school, and especially had they taken note of the lessons on Greek mythology, things might have ended differently. Sadly for them, that was not the case.

"Turn around," Tad said.

"Take my advice and take the gold," the leprechaun said.

"Turn around," Tad said again.

And so Plato O'Brien turned toward the twins. He was half–Irish leprechaun, descended from sea sprites, and half–Greek gorgon, descended from sea gods. Gorgons, of course, are so hideous that the sight of them can turn people to stone. Plato smiled a truly hideous yet still-charming smile and lifted his hat, freeing the green snakes that were his hair. The snakes wriggled and hissed at the twins. Being half-gorgon, Plato turned them only halfway to stone. Unfortunately, that half happened to be not their left side, or their right side, or their upper half, or their lower half. It was their outer half that grew rock hard as they flung their arms out and screamed in terror.

Tad and Rufus, on the outside, were now solid stone and horrifying to behold. On the inside, they were still human and very unhappy about the situation. But there was nothing they could do about it. Even their attempts to scream or to plea for help were absorbed by the solid, unmoving stone.

"Twins," Plato said, eyeing his newest decorations. "Now that's a treasure. They'll look splendid on either side of the path." He dragged the statues up the hill, one by one, then went back to sitting on the rock, admiring his pot of gold, enjoying the beautiful rainbow that touched the ground in front of him, and waiting to see what lovely treasure seekers came along next.

SNOWFLAKES

My brother and I are identical twins. Identical on the outside, that is. Inside, we are different in a lot of ways. I love art and music more than anything. Ryan loves science. This doesn't mean I hate science or Ryan hates art. It just means we have stuff we like the most. But Ryan got me started on a science project that could have made me famous.

It happened in December, during the first snowfall of the season. I was staring out the window, looking at the snow-covered branches I planned to sketch. Ryan was checking an app on his phone to get a reading from the weather station he'd built on the roof of our garage.

"We're like rock crystals on the outside, but snowflakes inside," he said.

I rolled my pencil between my fingers. "What do you mean?"

"Crystals that form under the same conditions will appear identical," he said. "That's us on the outside, right?"

"Right," I said. "Except I'm taller and better looking."

Ryan ignored the joke, which I'd probably made a thousand times, and went on. "No two snowflakes are alike. That's us on the inside."

I ignored the part about us and seized the part about snowflakes. "What do you mean?" I pointed out the window. "Look at them. There are billions, and they're all the same."

"Not if you take a close look." He pointed across the room, where his microscope sat on a shelf. "Each snowflake is unique. We learned that in school. Remember?"

"Nope. I guess I wasn't paying attention. And I'm not sure I believe you," I said.

"You have to," he said. "It's true."

"Prove it," I said.

Ryan shrugged. "I can't."

That stopped me cold. And, no, that wasn't a snowflake joke. I'd expected him to offer some kind of proof or admit he'd made the whole thing up just to mess with me.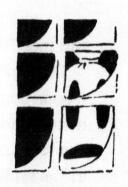

"What do you mean *you can't?*" I asked.

"You can't prove a law of science. Or any absolute statement," he said. "The only way to prove it would be to look at every single snowflake."

"That's impossible," I said. "Even if you started checking them right now, zillions of them have melted."

"Right," Ryan said. "Any absolute statement, like *all trout have gills* or *all dogs bark* can't be proven. You can just make it more and more likely to be true with every trout or dog you study."

"But some dogs don't bark," I said. I loved dogs, too. I'd done a report on them. I knew a lot about them.

Ryan flung his arm out. "Exactly!"

His shout startled me. I waited to see if he had more to say. He did.

"You gave me an example that showed I was wrong about dogs. It works that way for any rule. It just takes one counterexample to disprove it," he said.

It took me a moment to think that through. But I saw what he meant. "So all I have to do is find two snowflakes that are the same, and you'll be wrong," I said. "And I'll still be taller and better looking."

"Good luck with that," he said.

I grabbed his microscope. "Can I borrow this?"

"Help yourself."

I took the microscope out to the porch and held it so some snowflakes fell on the glass slide. Then I looked at them.

Wow. They were beautiful. And different. I wiped off the slide and caught a few more. They were also beautiful. And different. But I realized I had a problem. What if the first one I looked at was just like the fiftieth one or the five hundredth? I'd have no way or remembering all the patterns.

I put the microscope down and ran inside to get my sketch pad.

"How's it going?" Ryan asked, flashing me a smug grin.

"I'm just getting started," I said.

I went out, caught more flakes on the slide, and started sketching them.

It was fun at first. I never got tired of drawing. But I was getting cold standing out there. And my sketch pad was getting full.

"Maybe I should give up," I said to myself. I looked over my shoulder. Ryan was inside, nice and warm. He caught me staring, spread his hands, and mouthed the word *Well?*

I turned away and got back to work. I just had to find one counterexample.

But I started to wonder whether I was

wasting my time. "Ten more minutes, and I'm going inside," I said as I captured more specimens.

And there they were. I was so surprised, I just stared for a moment. Right on the slide,  side by side, I saw two snowflakes that were as identical as twins.

"Yes!" I shouted, leaping in the air. I spun toward the house.

"Ryan!" I screamed, shouting loudly enough that my voice could be heard through the window.

"What?" he shouted back.

"I found them."

He threw on his coat and came outside. "This better not be a joke."

I didn't even bother answering him. I just pointed at the microscope.

He leaned over, adjusted the focus, stared for a moment, then said, "Wow . . ." The word came out like a long sigh.

"Identical," I said.

"Yeah . . ."

I watched the mist flow from his mouth as he spoke the word. Then he clamped his mouth shut and backed away.

"What's wrong?" I asked.

He just pointed at the microscope. I leaned over and took a look. But deep inside, I already knew what had happened. There, on the slide, instead of identical snowflakes, I saw identical tiny blobs of water. Ryan's breath had melted the snowflakes.

"But you saw it," I said. "Right?"

"Right."

"So you know I proved you wrong. Right?"

"Right," he said. "But there's no evidence for the rest of the world. That's what really matters."

"Not to me," I said.

"It would to me," he said.

"And that just proves we're different in every way," I said.

"No," Ryan said. "I told you that you can't prove an—"

"An absolute," I said, cutting him

off and grinning a big enough smile to let him know I was joking. "How about we crystal-snowflake twins go get some identical mugs of hot chocolate?"

"Absolutely," he said.

And we did. Though mine was bigger and tastier.

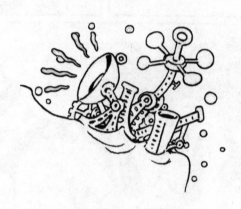

IN LIKE A LION

saw Serena Watkins sitting at the top of a hill near the playground. She had a pair of binoculars in her hands and a camera dangling from a strap around her neck. I hiked up the path to find out what was going on.

"Hi, Tammy," she said when I reached her. "Did you come to watch?"

"Watch what?"

"The lion," she said.

I had no idea what she was talking about. I waited.

"It's the first day of March," she explained.

I knew that. But I still had no clue what the

date had to do with Serena's decision to sit at the top of a hill. So I waited some more. Her next words didn't help all that much, either.

"My folks always say that March comes in like a lion and goes out like a lamb."

"That's just an expression," I told her. I'd heard it from my folks, too. "It means the weather is wild at the start of the month, because it's still winter, and tame at the end, because it's finally spring. There isn't a real lion."

"Wild, huh?" Serena smirked at me and pointed to the calm, cloudless, clear-blue sky. "I don't think so."

I guess she was right about that. A mild breeze ruffled our hair. I took a seat next to her on the hilltop. I didn't think a lion was going to come, but I liked hanging out with Serena.

She offered me the binoculars. "Want to take a look?"

"Sure." I looked. I saw houses, streets, cars, and kids. No lion. I handed the binoculars back. "Thanks."

We sat for a while. I didn't mind. The weather was nice.

"Hey, how do you know it will come from that way?" I finally asked, pointing in the direction we were facing.

She tapped her watch, which had a small compass on the band. "That's due east. Stuff moves east to west. The sun comes from the east. The new day comes from the east. March comes from the east. So will the lion."

"Makes sense," I said. "But wouldn't the lion come right when March started, like at midnight?"

"Lions like to sleep. They're just big cats," Serena said. "My cat sleeps a lot. Besides, I don't think the lion would want to get up in the dark unless it absolutely had to. I didn't see any reason for me to, either."

"I guess that makes sense, too," I said. Of

course, even though every part of what she said made sense, I didn't think that when you put all the parts together, you'd end up with a lion.

I was about to tell her that when I heard the roar from behind us. Serena and I leaped to our feet and spun around. We found ourselves facing a lion that had crept up the back side of the hill. Yup—a real, living and breathing, bushy-maned lion stood ten yards away from us.

"Lions are sneaky, too," I said. "They're hunters."

"That's a male," Serena said. "The females do the hunting."

"You also said the lion would come from the east," I reminded her. "I don't think you get to call yourself an expert on their behavior."

"How about if I say we turn around and run as fast as we can?" she asked.

"I'd definitely listen," I said.

We spun so we could run. And a bunch of things happened at once. As I looked back over

my shoulder, the lion crossed the distance im-
possibly fast. It leaped at us, roaring. I could
see nothing but teeth and feel hot lion breath
washing over me as if I were
leaning above a bubbling
pot of beef-barley soup.
At the same time the lion
leaped, the sky turned so
dark, I felt someone had pulled
the plug on the sun. Heavy clouds blew in
from the east, gray on the top and black on
the bottom.

I could feel the hair on my arms stand up
as lightning struck the leaping lion, knocking
it to the ground. Torrential rain fell, instantly
soaking us.

The lion got back up. I was glad he wasn't
hurt at all, but I was sad Serena and I were
about to be hurt in all kinds of ways.

Much to my relief, as a second bolt of lightning hit between us and the lion, he ran off
like a scared cat.

"I think I'll head home," I said. I was already so wet, there was no point running.

Serena sighed as she slipped her camera under her shirt. "I guess I'm not getting a photo of a lion today."

"Well, maybe in a month, you can get a good picture of the lamb," I said.

"That sounds like a much better idea," Serena said as we slogged our way down the hill toward what I hoped would be a wonderful spring.

THIN ICE

Almost everything about the skates was wrong. They were bright green with sparkles. They had neon-blue laces. And they had jagged teeth at the tips instead of a nice smooth curve.

They were Joe's mom's figure skates from twenty years ago.

The only thing that wasn't wrong about them was that they fit. And Joe needed skates. He had his brother's old hockey stick. He had a mouth guard from the one year he'd tried wrestling. But there wasn't any money for skates.

"You can't have new skates and dance lessons," his mom had said. "We just can't afford both right now."

"I know." Joe realized the lessons cost a lot. That didn't matter. He couldn't give them up. He loved to dance. But each time he walked past Krueger Pond and saw everyone slapping around hockey pucks and having a wonderful time, he felt a twinge of envy and a tug of sadness.

He hadn't skated in years, but he figured his sense of balance from dance would make it easy for him. He tried the skates out early one morning, when he knew nobody would be around except for a couple of college kids who liked to work on their speed skating before their classes started.

I guess I could at least buy new laces, he thought as he put the skates on and tied them tightly. Not that it would make all that much difference.

He got off the bench and walked the short

distance to the ice. After he'd stepped onto the slick surface with both feet, he stood for a moment, making sure he had his balance. Then he pushed off and glided toward the center of the pond.

Yeah, he thought *I can do this.* Within a few minutes, he was skating forward, backward, and in lazy circles, while a half dozen other skaters zipped around the edge of the lake at dizzying speeds.

Joe put on his own burst of speed, pretending to move a puck with an imaginary stick as he raced down the center of the frozen pond. The cold air felt great as it stroked his face. "I can't wait to play," he said.

Right after school, Joe grabbed his skates and went back to the pond. Sure enough, a group of kids had already gathered. Joe was glad to see they hadn't started a game yet. They were still slapping pucks around.

He skated over to them and said hi to Troy, the kid he knew best among the group.

"I didn't know you were into hockey," Troy said.

Joe shrugged. "It's been a while."

He heard someone laugh. Kids nudged each other and pointed at his feet. Joe felt his face grow warm. "Can I join in?" he asked.

"Sure," Troy said.

"Are you kidding?" Burly Andrews said. "We're not doing figure eights."

"Yeah, this isn't ice dancing," Burly's cousin Alvin said. He raised one leg, did a shaky circle, then slipped and fell, banging into the ice.

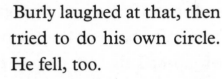

Burly laughed at that, then tried to do his own circle. He fell, too.

Everyone started laughing and falling down on purpose as they skated in a circle.

Joe sighed and started to skate away. But

another boom, way louder than the sound of someone falling, caused him to turn back.

Something was banging at the ice from underneath. Everyone backed away from the spot. Joe could see a thin circle had been carved there from all the skaters. He could also see something shadowy beneath the ice. The banging continued.

Then the ice broke, shattering up from the circle.

A creature, looking like a seal with gorilla arms and shark's teeth, clambered out of the hole.

Everyone turned and fled. Joe joined them. Above their screams, he heard another cry. He spun around and slid to a stop.

Burly had fallen again. The monster had reached him and grabbed him with one clawed hand.

"Help!" Burly screamed as the monster lifted him higher.

Joe didn't hesitate. He skated full speed

toward the monster. When he got close enough, he leaped in the air and extended one leg. He  went into a spin, just as he'd learned in dance class. As he came around full circle, he slashed the serrated tip of his right skate across the face of the monster.

It howled, dropped Burley, and clutched at its slashed cheek. Joe backed off, ready to make another attack if necessary. But the creature had obviously felt enough cold steel for one day. It dived back into the hole.

The other kids skated over and stared down at the opening in the ice.

Burly got up slowly. "You're amazing!" he said to Joe. "Thanks for saving me."

"Any time," Joe said. Then he laughed, because that was sort of a funny thing to say when someone just thanked you for saving them from a monster. "Though I hope not."

"I hope not, either," Burly said.

"Looks like we need to find another place to skate," someone said.

"We will," Troy said. "But we don't need to find another player. We've got a great new one." He patted Joe on the back.

"Those are kind of cool," someone said, pointing at Joe's skates.

The others agreed.

"No way!"

That's what Joe almost said. Instead, as he thought about his amazing leap and courage he didn't even know he had, he smiled and said, "Yeah. They are pretty great."

A SUCKER FOR VALENTINES

Hero.

Hoagie.

Grinder.

Po' boy.

Sub.

I could give you all five of those, and you'd still have just one thing. But it would be a tasty thing. Those are all names for a sandwich. Which one should you use? It depends where you live. I learned this because we move a lot. That's not a bad thing. It means I have all kinds of different experiences. My dad is in the army. We move at least once every three years. I'm used to it. I've lived in Connecticut, Texas, Georgia, and Utah. I've visited my grandparents in Florida and Illinois. And we've taken family trips to Arizona, Nevada, and Massachusetts.

In one place, what I call a water fountain, everyone called a *bubbler*. In another, they called any sort of fizzy drink a *Coke*, even if it was root beer or ginger ale. In some places, it's *soda*. In others, it's *pop*. I guess, somewhere, it's probably *soda pop*.

It's not weird. It's not wrong. It's just different. And maybe a bit confusing until you get used to it.

So I was only a little puzzled when I started at my new school a week before Valentine's Day and heard my new classmates talking about the party. They had a pretty cool rule. Every kid had to get something for every other kid in their class. Nobody got left out.

"It's a lot of fun, Portia," Danny Rodriguez told me. He's the first kid I got to know when I arrived. "Each of us gets to sit up front, one at a time. And we all give them their valentine."

"A card?" I asked. That's what we'd done in most of my schools.

"A card or a special treat," Cindy Sketz said.

Cindy was the second kid I made friends with. I knew three or four other kids, but I always take my time making friends at new schools. And in most schools, all the kids take time getting to know the new kid. But thanks to Cindy and Danny, I was just about to learn how to become super popular really quickly and also learn a strange new word. Okay, maybe it wasn't all that strange, but it was definitely different.

"What kind of treat?" I asked. I didn't want to bring the wrong thing. I'd feel silly if I showed up with cupcakes when everyone else brought candy bars. Or cabbages. Okay, that example was silly. But just like local words can be a surprise, you never know what the local customs are, and it's not *totally* impossible there's a place where kids give each other cabbages.

"It can be a sweet heart, a sour ball, or just about anything," Danny said.

"But we give the one kid we like best a sucker," Cindy said. "That's a tradition. Even my parents and grandparents did that when they were in school here."

"And the super best kid gets an all-day sucker," Danny said.

I knew what sweet hearts were, of course. Those are the littler candy hearts with stuff written on them. And I love sour balls—the sourer the better. I liked to get my mouth so puckered, I couldn't help whistling when I talked. But it took me a moment to figure out that *sucker* was just another word for *lollipop.* So the all-day sucker had to be those really huge lollipops that were as wide as a salad plate and usually made with spirals of different colors and flavors.

And I knew one important thing Dad

always told me: "People like it when you make them feel special." I decided I was going to make my whole class feel special. I'd give every one of them a sucker. No. Even better. I'd give each of them an all-day sucker! And it would be the best one I could find. I could just picture all my classmates grinning at me as I gave them their treats.

I walked through town on the way home and stopped at a candy store. That's where my plan almost ended. They had huge lollipops on the counter in a plastic bucket next to the cash register, but they weren't cheap. Buying enough for the whole class would take a lot more money than I had.

"Can I get my allowance for next week?" I asked my mom when she came home from work.

"Sure," she said.

"And the week after that?" I asked. Before she could answer, I said, "And maybe the next two or three weeks after that, too. Actually, three months' worth would be good."

"Are you buying a car?" she asked.

I laughed. Mom likes it when I laugh at her jokes. "No, it's for Valentine's Day."

"Are you planning a wedding?" she asked. "I know Valentine's Day is a popular date for people to get married, but if that's what's going on, you'll need at least a year or two of your allowance. Weddings are expensive."

"I want to buy huge lollipops for my class." I blurted out an explanation quickly enough to tell her everything before she could make another joke.

Happily, Mom understood why this was so important and offered to pay for the candy herself. "Just remember," she said as we headed for the candy store, "you can't buy friends."

"Yeah, but you can rent them," I said.

She frowned. But then she laughed when she realized I was kidding. Mom isn't the only one who can make a joke.

So I got twenty all-day suckers, put them in a large bag, and dragged them to school on Valentine's Day. I couldn't wait to see how surprised everyone would be when I gave each of them an all-day sucker.

But I started to get worried when I saw Danny outside of the school. He had a large bag, too. So did everyone in my class. Except for Cindy. She had *two* large bags and a big smile she flashed at me every time I looked in her direction.

I hoped my big surprise wasn't about to become no surprise at all when everyone gave out a bunch of all-day suckers.

Right after class started, our teacher, Ms. Maclatchy, said, "Portia, I want you to take the special spot, since you're new."

It turned out the special spot meant I was going last. That was great. My surprise would come at the end and be even more amazing. Danny was up first. I got in the back of the line and watched as each kid in front of me gave him a treat. Even though they all had large bags, the treats were small. Until it was my turn.

"Oooohhh . . . ," someone said as I pulled out the all-day sucker and gave it to Danny.

"Wow!"

"Awesome!"

"That's gigantic!"

Everyone was impressed. Especially Danny.

"Thanks for the lollipop!" he said.

I should have gotten worried then, but I was so glad I'd finally revealed my surprise that I wasn't paying much attention to the word he used.

The class got more and more impressed as I gave every single kid a huge lollipop. And I got more and more puzzled as they all pulled sweet hearts, sour balls, and other tiny treats from their bags and thanked me for the lollipop.

Finally, it was my turn. I sat on a chair in front of the class and held my hands out. Everyone lined up. I saw Danny and Cindy slip to the back of the line. I guess, just like me, they wanted to save the best for last. I was glad they'd picked me to get the special treat.

Delilah Schwartz, who was the first kid in line, opened her bag, reached in, fumbled around a bit like she was having a hard time grabbing my treat, and finally pulled a green blob out and plopped it in my hands.

I let out a gasp that nearly became a scream before I choked it down.

The thing Delilah had dropped into my hand was about the size of a baseball. But it sure didn't feel like a baseball. It was wet, soft, and slimy. And it wriggled!

I had a hard time believing what I saw, but there was no doubt. It was an octopus.

As I stared at it, the next kid gave me another one. Both creatures wrapped their tentacles around my wrists and clung to me with their slimy suckers.

Suckers!

Oh no . . .

Everything suddenly made sense.

I wanted to shake the octopuses off, but

they clung to me. As I sat there, more and more kids gave me octopuses and, for variety, some squid, piling them up in my hands and on my lap.

They were heaped up and clinging all over my body by the time Danny and Cindy reached me. They carried a big bag between them.

"We want to show you how much we like you," Danny said.

"Ready?" Cindy asked.

"I guess . . ." At this point, I didn't think things could get any worse. Naturally, I was wrong.

"On the count of three," Danny said as he and Cindy reached into the bag with both hands.

They counted. And then they pulled out an enormous octopus and plopped it on my head like a crown.

"All-day sucker!" Danny and Cindy said.

And it was. It clung to my head for the entire school day. That's about all I remember of

Valentine's Day, except maybe I let out some screams once in a while as the tentacles massaged my neck or explored my nostrils. And maybe I shuddered a bit.

I took the octopuses to the ocean on the way home and set them free. I had to admit, they were cute and friendly once I got used to them. But I was happy to get rid of them. And I was especially glad to say goodbye to my enormous all-day sucker. He might have been fond of me, but I never really felt attached to him.

ABOUT THE AUTHOR

DAVID LUBAR credits his passion for short stories to his limited attention span and bad typing skills, though he has been known to sit still and peck at the keyboard long enough to write a novel or chapter book now and then, including *Hidden Talents* (an ALA Best Book for Young Adults) and *My Rotten Life*, which is currently under development for a cartoon series. He lives in Nazareth, Pennsylvania, with his amazing wife, and not too far from his amazing daughter. In his spare time, he takes naps on the couch.

ABOUT THE
ILLUSTRATOR

BILL MAYER is absolutely amazing. Bill's crazy creatures, characters, and comic creations have been sought after for magazine covers, countless articles, and even stamps for the U.S. Postal Service. He has won almost every illustration award known to man and even some known to fish. Bill and his wife live in Decatur, Georgia. They have a son and three grandsons.